I0580493

To Noa

With a funnel
i can hear
noises over the
OCEAN...

Come on,
birdy friend,
i can carry
you on my
funnel!

I will be
your private
BUS...

At night,
I can see the Moon
and collect some
stars in my
funnel!

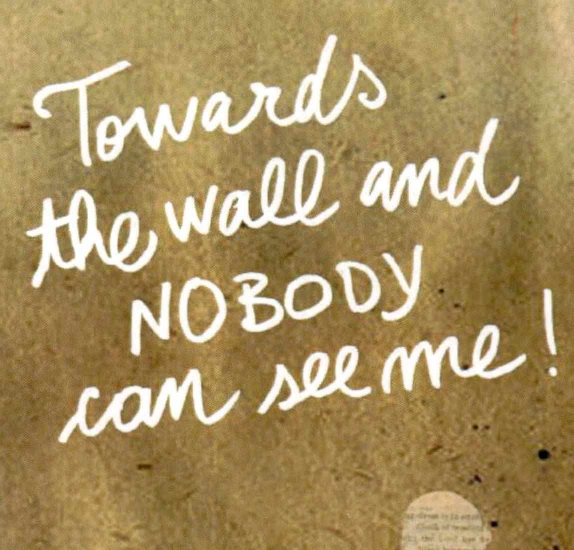

Towards the wall and NOBODY can see me!

A vase for fresh
flowers.
Please, check if
they match
my eyes.

A TV antenna
to get CAT
subtitles.
Enjoy !

When it rains, I have a private swimming pool!

"No bag?"
said the
greengrocer

"let's use your funnel
for your
oranges!"

A nobel cat of the 18th century
Let me introduce you to my King.

"It's so cold! What shall i do?
"Come, squirrel, and hide into
my funnel. It sure is cozy!"

We, funnel cats, can have
private conversations everywhere
just putting our cones
TOGETHER.

But … do you want to know a secret? The reason this cone is so SPECIAL to me?

Because it helps
me not focus on the
big, crazy world
around me.

Actually, it helps me
keep my focus on
the main thing
that's most important
to me:

you!

www.ingramcontent.com/pod-product-compliance
Lightning Source LLC
Chambersburg PA
CBRC092147180726
48295CB00011B/139